Desert Critter Friends

Spelling Bees

Mona Gansberg Hodgson
Illustrated by Chris Sharp

CPH
SAINT LOUIS

Dedicated to Nancy Jarrell, my English teacher at
Riverside Christian High School in Riverside,
California. With special thanks to Sherri
Crawford for her critique of this story.

Desert Critter Friends Series

Friendly Differences	*Jumping Jokers*
Thorny Treasures	*Campout Capers*
Sour Snacks	*Sticky Statues*
Smelly Tales	*Goofy Glasses*
Clubhouse Surprises	*Crabby Critters*
Desert Detectives	*Spelling Bees*

Scripture quotations taken from the HOLY BIBLE, NEW INTERNATIONAL VERSION®.
NIV®. Copyright © 1973, 1978, 1984 by International Bible Society. Used by
permission of Zondervan Publishing House. All rights reserved.

Text copyright © 2000 Mona Gansberg Hodgson
Illustration copyright © 2000 Concordia Publishing House
Published by Concordia Publishing House
3558 S. Jefferson Avenue, St. Louis, MO 63118-3968
Manufactured in the United States of America

Library of Congress Cataloging-in-Publication Data

Hodgson, Mona Gansberg, 1954–
    Spelling bees / Mona Gansberg Hodgson ; illustrated by Chris Sharp.
        p.   cm. — (Desert Critter Friends ; bk 12)
    Summary: Because Jamal the rabbit fails to promptly clean up his spilled
milkshake in the clubhouse, he and his friends face a problem when they
want to use it. Additional text explains that God wants us to be responsible for our actions.
    ISBN 0-570-07075-9
    [1. Responsibility—Fiction. 2. Behavior—Fiction. 3. Rabbits—Fiction.
4. Desert animals—Fiction. 4. Christian life—Fiction.] I. Sharp, Chris,
1954- ill. II. Title.
    PZ7.H6649 Sp 2000
    [E]—dc21   98-050661

1 2 3 4 5 6 7 8 9 10   09 08 07 06 05 04 03 02 01 00

Jamal, the jackrabbit, looked out at the noon sun. "Whew! It's hot out!" he said to himself. He wiped his forehead with his bandana. Then he tied it around his neck.

He hop-hop-hopped to a clump of grass under the shade of a cottonwood tree. "Boy! If I didn't have a milkshake mess to clean up at the clubhouse, I wouldn't be out here in this heat."

Jamal munched on a mouthful of grass before going to the clubhouse.

SCREEEEECH! Suddenly his friend Bert, the roadrunner, came to a dust-flying stop right in front of him. "Hey, Jamal," he said.

"Hi, Bert!" Jamal said. "I'm glad you have good brakes in that tail of yours." He laughed.

"Me too!" Bert said, laughing.

"Want to help me practice for the Desert Critter Spelling Bee?" Bert pulled a book out of his backpack. "Here's my dictionary (*dic-shun-air-e*)." He handed it to Jamal.

"Sure," Jamal said. "Where do I start?"

"I marked the page with a leaf," Bert said. "Give me the word 'explore.' " Bert thought hard. He paced back and forth. Back and forth. Back and forth.

Jamal opened to the right page. Then he ate the leaf. "Okay," he said. "Spell 'explore.' "

"EXPLORE," Bert said. "E-X-P-L-O-R-E!" He zoomed over to Jamal.

"That's right!" Jamal said. "E-x-p-l-o-r-e. I hope I get the word 'FUNNY'—F-U-N-N-E." He jumped up and down.

"I just remembered the joke you told at the ice-cream social yesterday." Bert laughed. "You are funny. But I think the word ends with 'Y.' F-U-N-N-Y. Did you get your milkshake mess cleaned up?"

9

"Not yet, but I will before tonight," Jamal said. He flipped the dictionary pages until he found the word "funny." "You're right," he said. "It is F-U-N-N-Y. It's a good thing we're practicing."

Bert said, "Now all we need is to
get the words at the spelling bee
that we know how to spell." He
laughed. "I'd better get going. I
have some exploring to do." Bert
pulled his backpack on. "See you
TONIGHT. T-O-N-I-G-H-T!"

"Okay." Jamal jump-jump-jumped into the air. "See you at SUNSET. S-U-N-S-E-T."

Bert pulled his cap down on his head. Bert zoom-zoom-zoomed away.

Jamal frowned as he thought about his mess at the desert critter clubhouse. He had laughed so hard that he had knocked over a milkshake just as everyone was leaving. It was his job to clean up his own mess. And he had promised Myra, the quail, that he would clean it up.

Jamal looked up at the sun. It was only early afternoon. "If I go to the clubhouse right now, I can clean up my milkshake mess before my friends get there for the spelling bee," he said to himself. He didn't really feel like doing it, but Jamal

jump-jump-jumped along the path
to the clubhouse. His big ears
flopped in the breeze.

"Hi, Jamal!" called Toby and
Wanda. The cottontails came
hopping toward him on the path.

15

"Hi, Jamal," Wanda said.
"We're going to the river for a
picnic."

Toby held up a basket. "We
have a lot to eat in here," he said.
"Do you want to come?"

16

"Well," Jamal said. First, he thought about his milkshake mess. Then he thought about how much he liked picnics. "Sure. I'll come," he shouted. "A picnic sounds like fun. *Then* I'll clean up my mess at the clubhouse."

Jamal, Toby, and Wanda hopped to the riverbank together. "Hey," Toby said. "Here's a shady tree we can sit under!"

"Cool!" Wanda said. She and Jamal spread out the big blanket. As the three friends ate their picnic lunch, they took turns practicing for the spelling bee.

"I'm STUFFED! S-T-U-F-F-E-D!" Toby said.

"Me too!" Jamal said as he yawned. "I feel like taking a short NAP. N-A-P!"

"Good idea!" Wanda and Toby agreed. And in a few minutes the sleepy rabbits were snoring.

Jamal woke up first. "Oh no!" he shouted.

Toby rubbed his sleepy eyes.
Wanda s-t-r-e-t-c-h-e-d! "What's
wrong?" they asked.

"It's evening," Jamal said. "I
need to get to the clubhouse!"

"Thanks for the picnic," he said
as he hop-hop-hopped away.

"Oh no!" Jamal said as he hopped even faster. "The spelling bee starts at sunset. It's almost sunset now, and I haven't cleaned up the milkshake mess!"

As Jamal got closer to the clubhouse, he saw his friends standing outside the door. They didn't look very happy. Jamal thought he heard a buzzing sound. *BUZZZZ! BUZZZZ!*

Jamal saw Myra frowning at him.

Lenny, the pack rat, swatted the air with his long skinny tail. Nadine, the javelina, snorted like a pig when Jamal hopped up.

Jamal scratched his head. Why weren't his friends in the clubhouse?

"Get away!" Myra shouted. She swatted at something in the air with her wing.

"Duck!" Lenny called. "Here come some more!"

BUZZZZ! BUZZZZ! Jamal could really hear it now. "Hey, what's going on?" he asked.

"*SNORT! SNORT!*" said Nadine, the javelina. "Hungry bees are filling the clubhouse!" she shouted.

"Look!" Lenny said. "They're coming from everywhere! It's all your fault!" He took another swing at the bees with his tail.

"Why are there bees at our spelling bee?" Jamal asked. He jump-jump-jumped up and down. Up and down. Up and down. "And why is that my fault?"

"It's your fault because you didn't clean up your milk-shake mess yesterday," Myra said. "It was your job. It was your responsibility (*re-spon-si-bil-i-tee*)." *BUZZZZ. BUZZZZ.* Myra flapped her wings to scare away bees buzzing toward the clubhouse.

Jamal gulped. "MY mess brought the bees to our spelling bee?" he asked.

"Yes!" Myra said. "This never would have happened if you had been responsible and thought about what might happen if you didn't do your job."

"LOOK OUT!" Lenny yelled. "Here come some more! They're filling the clubhouse!" The buzzing got louder and LOUDER. *BUZZZZ. BUZZZZ!*

"I didn't feel like cleaning it up yesterday," Jamal said. "I was going to clean it up this afternoon. But ... " Jamal swatted at the bees with his big back foot. "I didn't think about bees liking a spilled milkshake. I was coming to clean it up now."

"It's too late now," Nadine said with a grunt. "The clubhouse is full of a gazillion buzzing bees. And that's a lot of bees!"

Bert zoomed up and tipped his head. "What's all that buzzing about?" he asked.

"As you can see, there are bees at our spelling bee!" Lenny shouted over the buzzing.

"Sounds like T-R-O-U-B-L-E!" Bert said. "That's what bees in the clubhouse spell. TROUBLE!"

Jamal frowned. "If I had done my job, even when I didn't feel like it, the bees never would have come," he said.

Taylor, the tortoise, strolled up. "Bees took over our clubhouse," Jamal told him. "Do you have any ideas?"

BUZZZZ! BUZZZZ! Taylor's bald head disappeared into his shell. "Yes, I do," he mumbled. "Let's do nothing."

"Do you mean N-O-T-H-I-N-G, NOTHING?" Myra asked. "What kind of an idea is that?"

Taylor poked his head out of his shell. "I read that bees don't like to be out at night. They'll probably fly out of the clubhouse and go home when it gets dark."

"But they really like that old milkshake," Jamal said. "We may never have our spelling bee if we do nothing!" *BUZZZZ! BUZZZZ!*

Rosie, the skunk, strolled up behind Jamal. "Sounds like we have bees in our clubhouse!" she said. "You want me to go in there and spray them with my skunk spray?"

"Great idea!" Jamal said. "That stinky stuff will make them leave." He laughed.

Bert paced back and forth, thinking hard. "I don't think that's a good idea, Rosie," he said. "That would make the clubhouse stink!"

"It's almost dark!" Taylor said. "See the shadows on the clubhouse?"

Just then Jamal ducked his head. "Look out!" he yelled. "Here they come—out of the clubhouse!" The buzzing got louder and LOUDER. *BUZZZZ. BUZZZZ!*

The desert critter friends all ducked. *BUZZZZ! BUZZZZ!* The bees flew right over the top of them.

Bert carefully peeked inside the clubhouse. "I don't see any more," he said.

"Whew!" Jamal said. "I'm really sorry, everyone. Doing other things instead of cleaning up my

mess was not a loving thing to do.
Will you forgive me?"

"We forgive you," his friends
said.

"We'll even help you clean it up, so we can get on with our spelling bee!" Myra said.

Jamal smiled at his friends. "Thanks, everyone. I never knew bees could spell," he said.

"Bees can spell?" his friends asked.

"Sure," Jamal said. "Bert says bees are great at spelling T-R-O-U-B-L-E. TROUBLE!"

They all laughed and followed the jumping Jamal into the clubhouse.

God loves you so much that He sent His Son, Jesus, to die for you. We love others because He first loved us. Ask God to help you show your love by being responsible (even when you don't feel like it).

Each one should carry his own load.
Galatians 6:5

Hi, kids!

The Bible teaches us that responsibility and obedience grow out of love. Here is a list of words about being responsible. Match the right word with the right sentence.

love   **trusted**

promises   **truth**

right

You are being responsible when you tell the __ __ __ __ __.

You exercise responsible behavior when you choose to do what is __ __ __ __ __.

Responsibility grows out of __ __ __ __

You show you are responsible when you can be __ __ __ __ __ __ __ to do your job.

You show you are responsible when you keep your __ __ __ __ __ __ __ __.

For Parents and Teachers:

Jamal didn't feel like cleaning up the mess he had made. Sound like any kids (or adults) you know? He gave in to his feelings and the distractions around him and put off doing his job. Because he neglected his job, Jamal and his friends faced inconvenience and even trouble when a swarm of bees moved into their clubhouse.

We, kids and adults alike, aren't so different from Jamal in this story. Often we do not understand what effect our actions or neglect will have on others. We place ourselves and our own desires before others.

Just as we sometimes struggle with our own responsibilities, children also face plenty of distractions that would draw them away from their chores, commitments, and convictions. Cleaning their room, clearing the dinner table, or being a champion for what is right isn't nearly as inviting as watching a video, riding a bike, or being accepted by "popular" kids.

Help your children to see that responsibility is the God-given ability to respond in love to others for what He has given to us through Jesus. Use Jamal's story to help them learn that carrying out responsibility is a way to show love to others. We choose to be responsible and place others first because God has shown His ultimate love to us through Jesus. While consequences may exist for neglecting responsibility, enable your children to understand that responsibility requires self-discipline and that they can turn to God for help.

Here are some questions you can use as discussion starters to help your children understand these concepts.

Discussion Starters

1. What does the story say Jamal did at the ice-cream social?

2. Why didn't Jamal clean up the spilled milk-shake right after he made the mess? Have you ever made a mess that you didn't feel like cleaning up? What happened?

3. Jamal was on his way to the clubhouse to clean up the mess when he saw his friends Toby and Wanda. What did he do instead of cleaning up his mess?

4. What happened at the clubhouse because Jamal didn't clean up his milkshake mess?

5. Have you ever chosen to do something else when you had a job to do? Did it cause trouble for anyone? If you are sorry, ask God to forgive you. If you didn't do what your parent or teacher asked you to do, ask that person to for-give you too.

Pray together. Thank God for showing His love for you by sending His Son to be your Savior. Thank Him for always keeping His promises. Ask Him to help you learn to be responsible. Ask God to help you keep your promises. Ask Him to help you do your jobs even when you don't feel like it.

God helps us to take care of our responsibilities. What are some of the things you can be responsible for? Tell me on these lines.

_____

_____

_____

_____

_____